Owls

by JoAnn Early Macken

Reading consultant: Susan Nations, M.Ed.,
author/literacy coach/consultant

WEEKLY READER

EARLY LEARNING LIBRARY

Please visit our web site at: www.earlyliteracy.cc
For a free color catalog describing Weekly Reader® Early Learning Library's list
of high-quality books, call 1-877-445-5824 (USA) or 1-800-387-3178 (Canada).
Weekly Reader® Early Learning Library's fax: (414) 336-0164.

Library of Congress Cataloging-in-Publication Data

Macken, JoAnn Early, 1953–
    Owls / JoAnn Early Macken.
       p. cm. — (Animals that live in the forest)
    Includes bibliographical references and index.
    ISBN 0-8368-4484-X (lib. bdg.)
    ISBN 0-8368-4491-2 (softcover)
    1. Owls—Juvenile literature. I. Title.
  QL696.S8M24   2005
  598.9'7—dc22   2004057225

This edition first published in 2005 by
Weekly Reader® Early Learning Library
330 West Olive Street, Suite 100
Milwaukee, WI 53212 USA

Art direction: Tammy West
Cover design and page layout: Kami Koenig
Picture research: Diane Laska-Swanke

Picture credits: Cover, p. 5 © Tom and Pat Leeson; p. 7 © Alan & Sandy
Carey; p. 9 © Rob & Ann Simpson/Visuals Unlimited; pp. 11, 17 © Joe McDonald/
Visuals Unlimited; p. 13 © Michael H. Francis; pp. 15, 19, 21 © Dave Welling

Printed in the United States of America

1 2 3 4 5 6 7 8 9 09 08 07 06 05

Note to Educators and Parents

Reading is such an exciting adventure for young children! They are beginning to integrate their oral language skills with written language. To encourage children along the path to early literacy, books must be colorful, engaging, and interesting; they should invite the young reader to explore both the print and the pictures.

Animals That Live in the Forest is a new series designed to help children read about forest creatures. Each book describes a different forest animal's life cycle, eating habits, home, and behavior.

Each book is specially designed to support the young reader in the reading process. The familiar topics are appealing to young children and invite them to read — and re-read — again and again. The full-color photographs and enhanced text further support the student during the reading process.

In addition to serving as wonderful picture books in schools, libraries, homes, and other places where children learn to love reading, these books are specifically intended to be read within an instructional guided reading group. This small group setting allows beginning readers to work with a fluent adult model as they make meaning from the text. After children develop fluency with the text and content, the book can be read independently. Children and adults alike will find these books supportive, engaging, and fun!

— Susan Nations, M.Ed., author, literacy coach,
and consultant in literacy development

In spring, a female owl lays round, white eggs. Baby owls hatch from the eggs. Their mother keeps the babies, or **owlets**, warm. Their father brings them food.

In a few weeks, the owlets grow feathers. Their gray or brown color helps the young owls hide. They cannot fly, but they **perch**, or sit, on branches. By fall, the owls are full grown.

Most owls do not build their own nests. Some owls use holes in trees. Some owls use old nests from other birds.

Owls hunt and eat small animals, or **prey**. They eat their prey whole. Later, they throw up the bones and fur.

Owls have large, round heads. They have flat faces and big eyes. Owls can see very well at night.

Owls can hear very well, too. They find and chase their prey by sound. Most owls' ears are slits or holes on the sides of their heads.

Special feathers help owls fly quietly. The feathers have soft edges. Other animals cannot hear owls fly.

An owl has four toes on each foot. Each toe has a sharp **talon**, or claw. The owl uses its talons for hunting.

Most owls are active at night. During the day, they hide. Owls are at home in the forest.

Glossary

owlets — baby owls

perch — to sit on

prey — animals that are hunted and eaten by other animals

talon — claw

For More Information

Books

Guess Who Swoops. Sharon Gordon (Benchmark Books)

Owls. Welcome to the World of Animals (series). Diane Swanson (Gareth Stevens)

Owls and their Homes. Animal Habitats (series). Deborah Chase Gibson (PowerKids Press)

Owls: Flat-Faced Flyers. Adele D. Richardson (Bridgestone)

Web Sites

Owls
www.mbr-pwrc.usgs.gov/id/framlst/infocenter .html#Strigidae
Pictures and facts about owls

23

Index

About the Author

JoAnn Early Macken is the author of two rhyming picture books, *Sing-Along Song* and *Cats on Judy*, and six other series of nonfiction books for beginning readers. Her poems have appeared in several children's magazines. A graduate of the M.F.A. in Writing for Children and Young Adults program at Vermont College, she lives in Wisconsin with her husband and their two sons. Visit her Web site at www.joannmacken.com.